THIS BOOK BELONGS TO:

_____

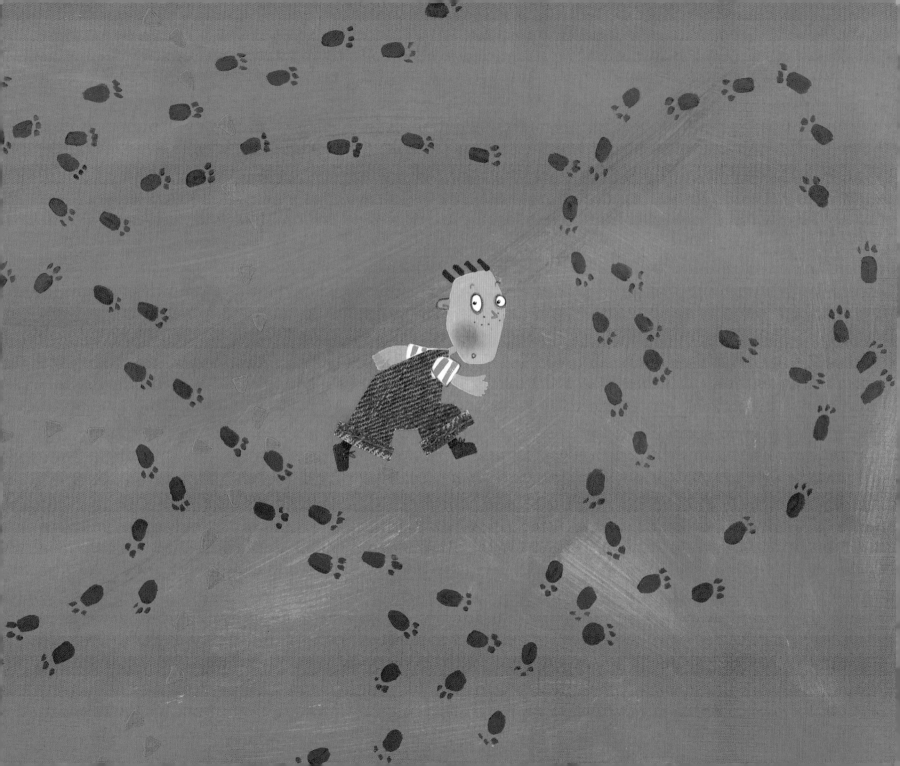

For my beloved granddaughters, Alexandra and Kelli,
who introduced me to the original "mad dog".

With special thanks to Sue Tarsky
who was the first to believe. — M. U.

For all my Monks and Tobin relatives in America. — L. M.

PUFFIN BOOKS

Published by the Penguin Group
Penguin Books Ltd, 80 Strand, London WC2R 0RL, England
Penguin Putnam Inc., 375 Hudson Street, New York, New York 10014, USA
Penguin Books Australia Ltd, 250 Camberwell Road, Camberwell, Victoria 3124, Australia
Penguin Books Canada Ltd, 10 Alcorn Avenue, Toronto, Ontario, Canada M4V 3B2
Penguin Books India (P) Ltd, 11 Community Centre, Panchsheel Park, New Delhi – 110 017, India
Penguin Books (NZ) Ltd, Cnr Rosedale and Airborne Roads, Albany, Auckland, New Zealand
Penguin Books (South Africa) (Pty) Ltd, 24 Sturdee Avenue, Rosebank 2196, South Africa

Penguin Books Ltd, Registered Offices: 80 Strand, London WC2R 0RL, England

www.penguin.com

First published in the USA by G. P. Putnam's Sons 2000
Published in Great Britain by Viking 2001
Published in Puffin Books 2002
10 9 8 7 6 5 4 3 2

Text copyright © Myron Uhlberg, 2000
Illustrations copyright © Lydia Monks, 2000
All rights reserved

The moral right of the author and illustrator has been asserted

Set in Malloy

Manufactured in China

British Library Cataloguing in Publication Data
A CIP catalogue record for this book is available from the British Library

ISBN 0–140–56799–2

MAD DOG McGRAW

MYRON UHLBERG

ILLUSTRATIONS BY LYDIA MONKS

PUFFIN BOOKS

I hate Mad Dog McGraw!

He barks like crazy, and he chases me.

He growls at trucks.

He snaps at clouds.

He barks at rain.

He shows his teeth to the wind.

He is such a mean dog.

The postman is afraid to
leave the post next door.

The milkman won't deliver their milk.
The paper boy throws their paper.

And when I see Mad Dog, I go the other way.
He is such a mean dog.

"I need stilts," I tell Mum. "Mad Dog tries to bite me."

"But, my dear, you don't know how to walk on stilts."

"I'll learn fast."

I find two old broom handles and make stilts.

I practise all week.
I'm ready for Mad Dog McGraw.

Here he comes.
He snaps.
He yelps.
He jumps.
But he can't reach me.
I've tricked Mad Dog McGraw!

Then my left stilt gets
caught in a crack.

Mad Dog McGraw chases me home.
I think I can hear him laughing in between
his barks.
He is such a mean dog.

"I need an umbrella," I tell Mum. "I'm going to sail right over Mad Dog McGraw."

"But, sweetheart, you can't fly."

"I'll learn fast." I practise all week. On Saturday, there's a strong wind blowing. I grab my umbrella. I'm ready for Mad Dog McGraw.

The wind is gusting. I open my umbrella and off I go.

Mad Dog spots me.

He hops.

He skips.

He jumps.

But he can't reach me.

I've tricked Mad Dog McGraw!

Then the wind stops.

Mad Dog McGraw chases me home.
I'm sure he's laughing again.

He is
such a
mean
dog.

"I need a cat,"
I tell Mum.

"But, darling,
we haven't
got a
cat."

"I'll find a stray."

Dad and I put down a saucer of milk.
Soon I have a cat. I call her Bait.

Bait and I tiptoe past Mad Dog McGraw's house.
Mad Dog gnashes those teeth.

Mad Dog leaps.

Bait purrs.

Bait licks Mad Dog's face.
Mad Dog nuzzles Bait.

Mad Dog chases me home.
This time I know he's laughing.

He is such a mean dog.

Mum is waiting for me.

"Well, Mum,
   that didn't work.
   Mad Dog is still mean."

"I wonder why?"
   Mum says.

I think about it.
And then
I think
a bit more.
Tricks don't seem to work.

All night I think about it. And then
I remember what happened with Bait.
Now I get it.
I'm learning fast.

Next morning, I go straight to Mad Dog McGraw's house.
I know I don't need stilts, or an umbrella, or Bait.

I kneel down.
I don't know who's more surprised,
Mad Dog or me.

I smile and hold out
a dog biscuit.

Mad Dog comes closer.
He sniffs.
He sniffs a bit more.
He looks at me and takes the treat.
He comes even closer.

He sniffs me.

He sniffs a bit more.

He sits, and I rub his head.
He licks my hand.

I know absolutely for sure that
Mad Dog is smiling.

I stand.
Mad Dog McGraw stands.
I walk home.

Mad Dog McGraw follows,
with Bait not far behind.

I think he is such a great dog.

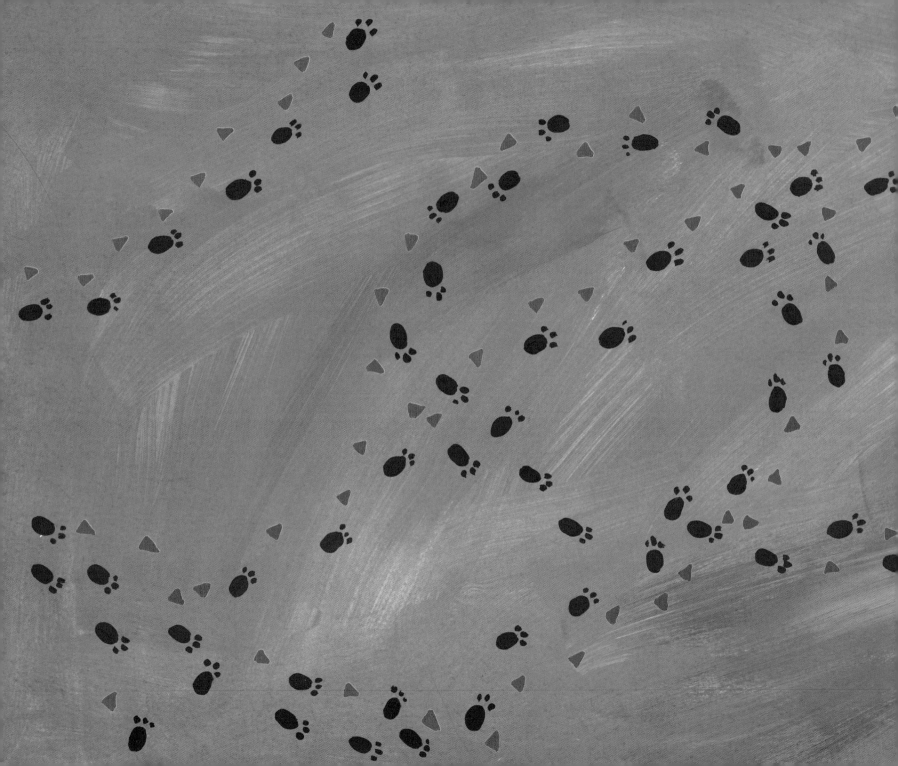